THIS CANDLEWICK BOOK BELONGS TO:

_____

_____

_____

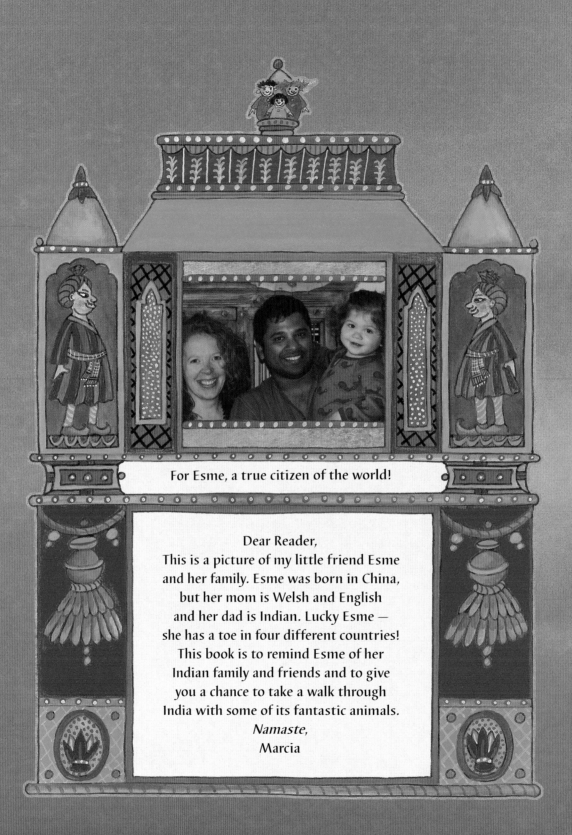

For Esme, a true citizen of the world!

Dear Reader,
This is a picture of my little friend Esme
and her family. Esme was born in China,
but her mom is Welsh and English
and her dad is Indian. Lucky Esme —
she has a toe in four different countries!
This book is to remind Esme of her
Indian family and friends and to give
you a chance to take a walk through
India with some of its fantastic animals.
*Namaste,*
Marcia

# The Elephant's Friend
## and
## Other Tales
## from
## Ancient India

retold and illustrated by
## Marcia Williams

CANDLEWICK PRESS

# The Elephant's Friend

Once upon a time, there was an elephant who lived in the palace stables.

He was the king's favorite elephant, so he was always well fed and cared for.

Outside the palace walls, a dog lay in the dirt—uncared for and starving.

He could smell the rice fed to the elephant, and his poor tummy rumbled.

One lucky day, the dog managed to slip through the palace gates.
Once inside, he followed the scent of the warm rice to the elephant's stable.

From then on, the dog enjoyed the rice that dropped from the elephant's mouth.

At first the skinny dog went unnoticed. But the more he ate, the fatter he grew!

So, who are you?

Dog!

And soon the elephant couldn't help but notice his uninvited companion!

Pleasure to meet you, Dog.

Likewise!

Far from being angry, the elephant was rather pleased to have some company.

Friendship and food!

That's all a body needs in life.

The two quickly became good friends, and the elephant shared both his stable and his food with the dog. As for the dog, he never left the elephant's side, day or night.

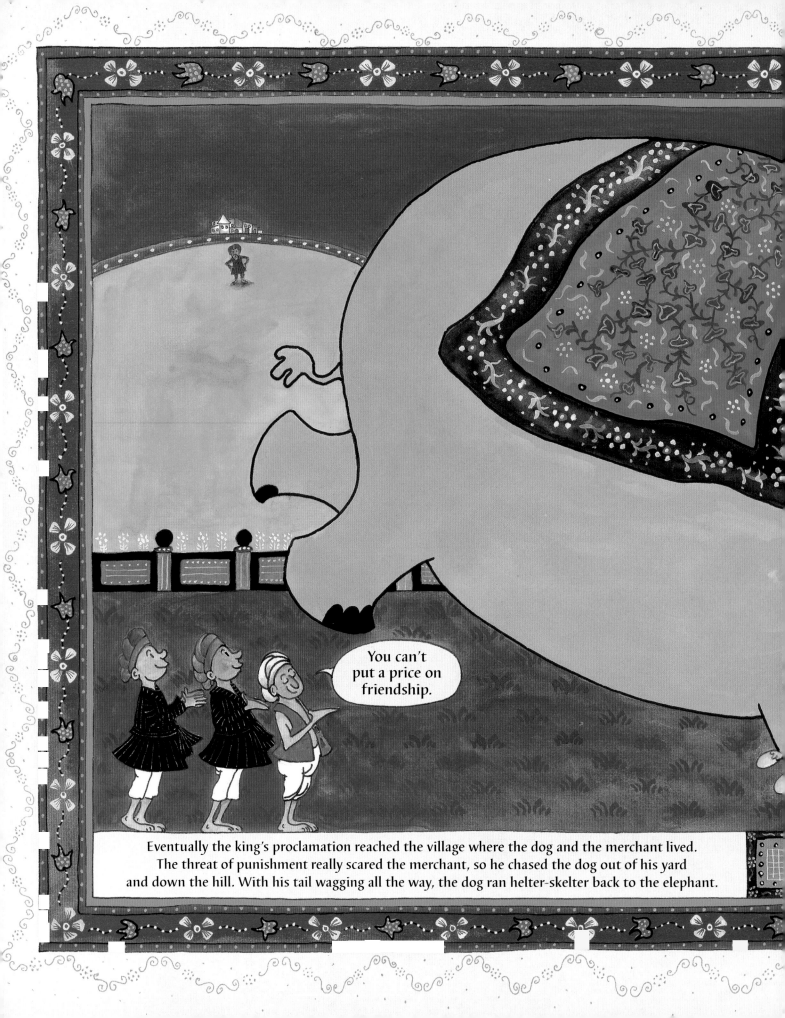

You can't put a price on friendship.

Eventually the king's proclamation reached the village where the dog and the merchant lived. The threat of punishment really scared the merchant, so he chased the dog out of his yard and down the hill. With his tail wagging all the way, the dog ran helter-skelter back to the elephant.

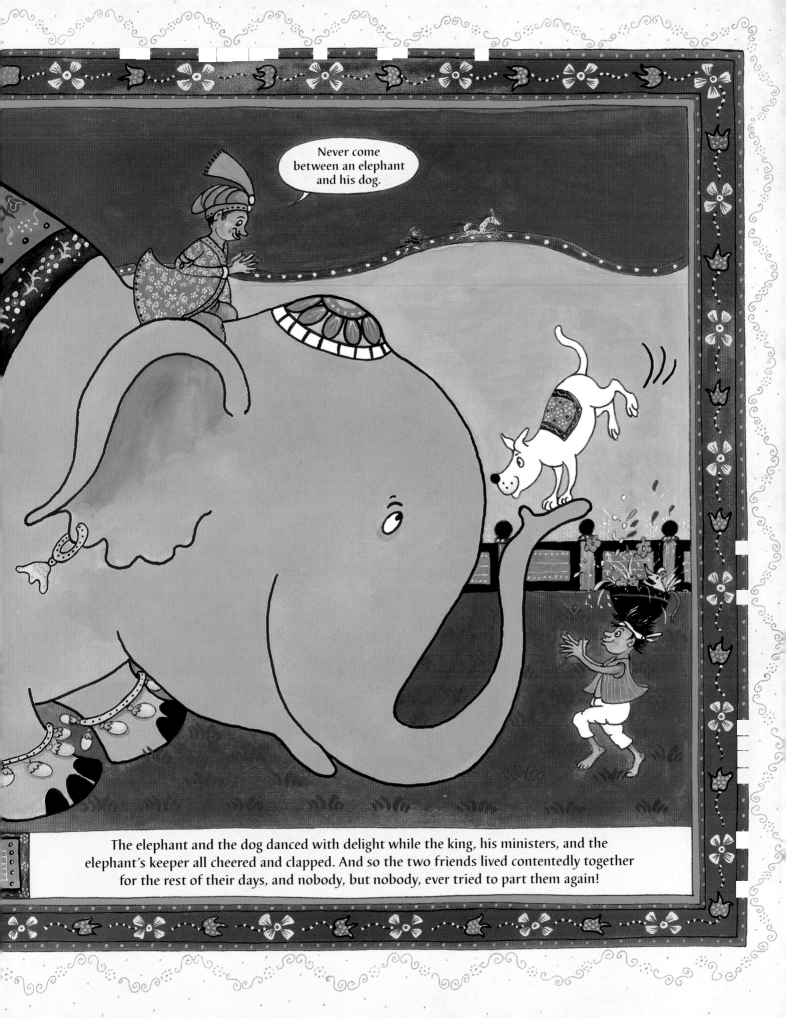

The elephant and the dog danced with delight while the king, his ministers, and the elephant's keeper all cheered and clapped. And so the two friends lived contentedly together for the rest of their days, and nobody, but nobody, ever tried to part them again!

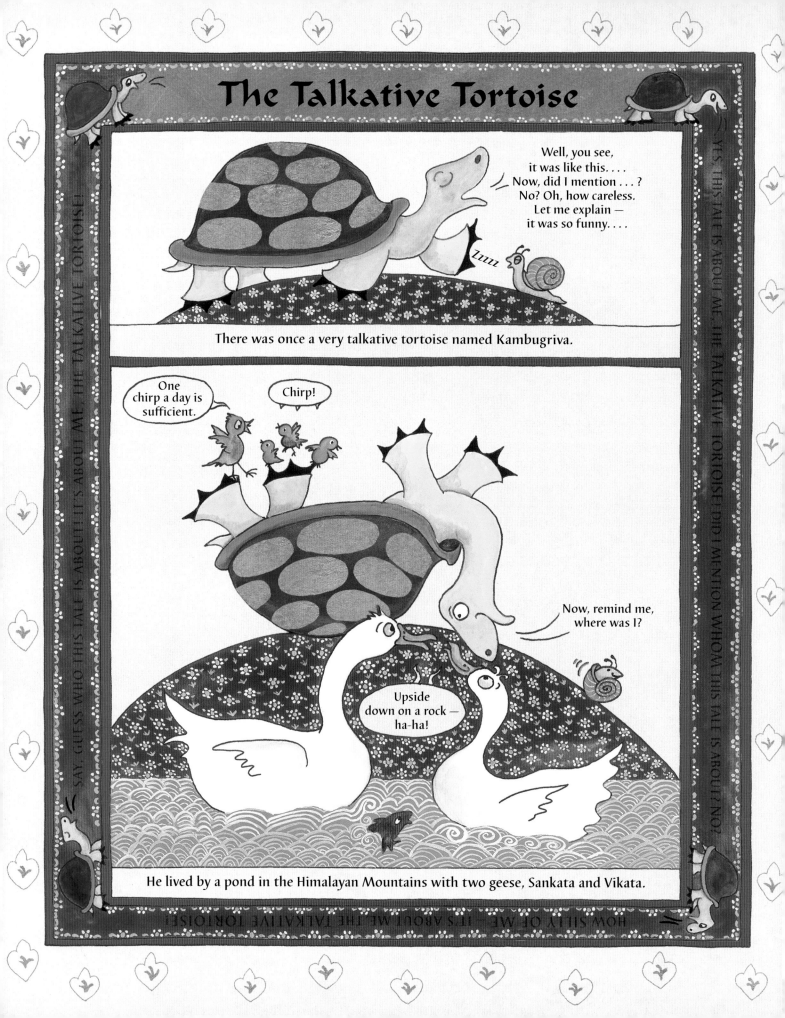

# The Talkative Tortoise

There was once a very talkative tortoise named Kambugriva.

He lived by a pond in the Himalayan Mountains with two geese, Sankata and Vikata.

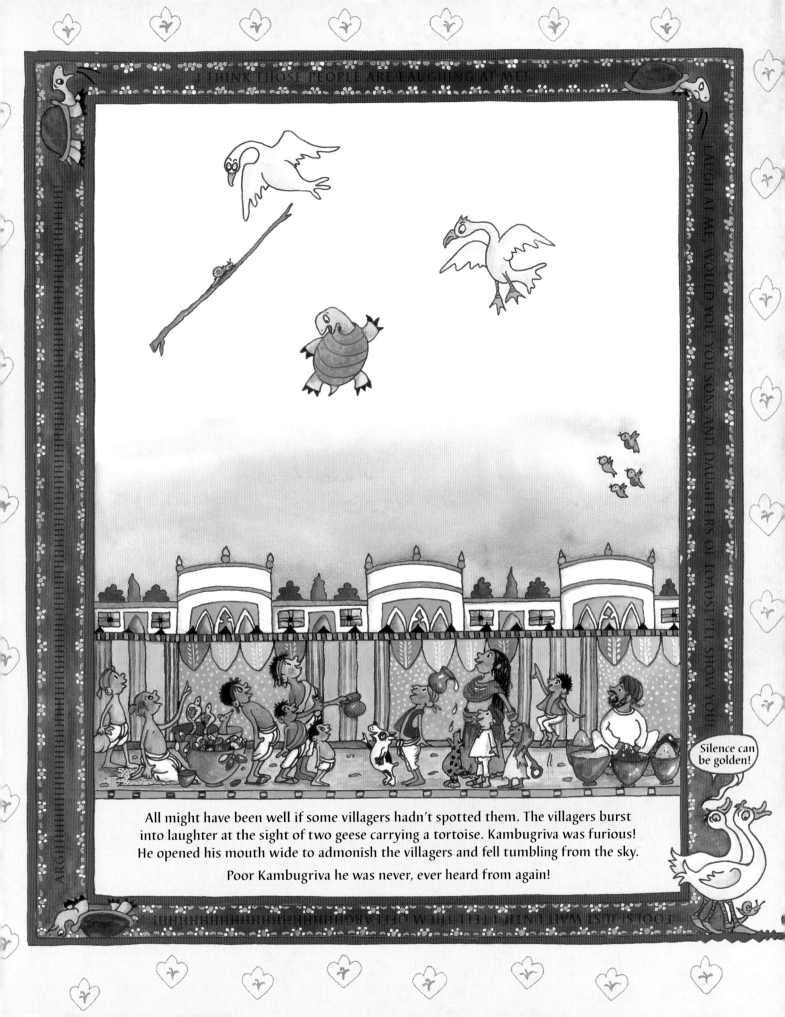

All might have been well if some villagers hadn't spotted them. The villagers burst into laughter at the sight of two geese carrying a tortoise. Kambugriva was furious! He opened his mouth wide to admonish the villagers and fell tumbling from the sky.

Poor Kambugriva he was never, ever heard from again!

# The Wise Little Pebet

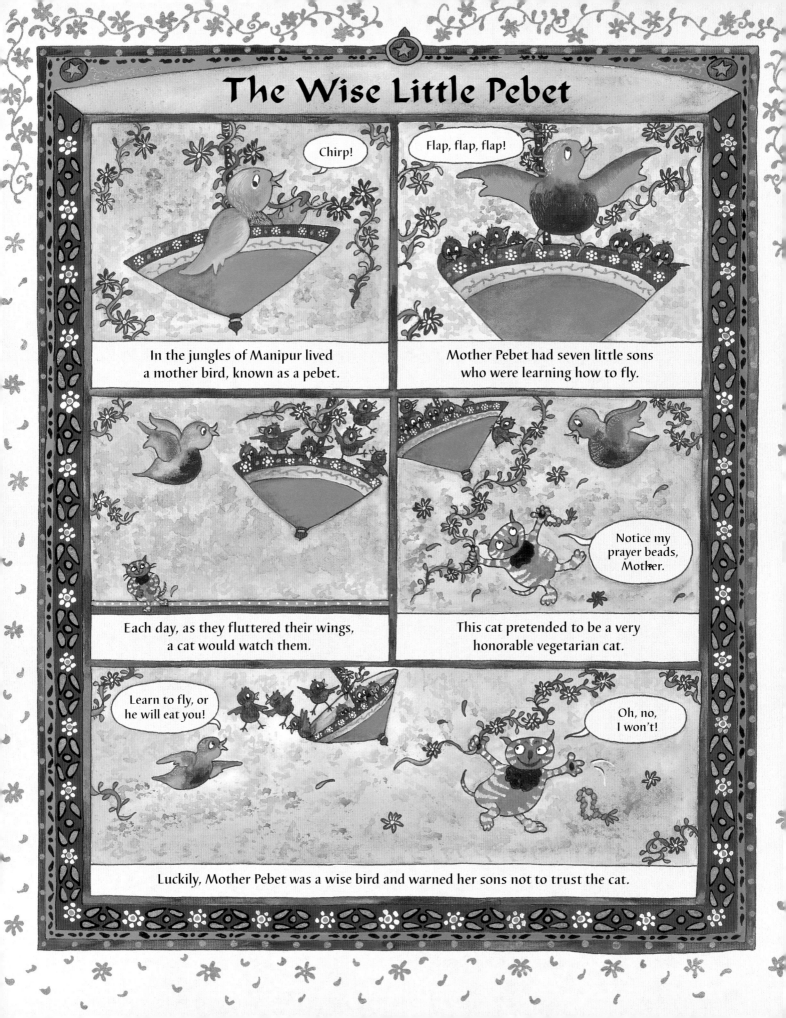

In the jungles of Manipur lived
a mother bird, known as a pebet.

Mother Pebet had seven little sons
who were learning how to fly.

Each day, as they fluttered their wings,
a cat would watch them.

This cat pretended to be a very
honorable vegetarian cat.

Luckily, Mother Pebet was a wise bird and warned her sons not to trust the cat.

All her sons soared into the sky except the very youngest, who failed to take off.

He tried and he tried and he tried, but he just couldn't make it.

So Little Pebet was caught in the claws of the hungry cat! The cat was just about to pop Little Pebet into his mouth when Mother Pebet suggested he would taste better if his sticky feathers were washed.

# The Golden Swan

Once upon a time, there was a swan with feathers made of the purest gold.
The swan lived on a fine pond and was rich in both food and friends.

Close by the pond, there lived a poor mother with her two daughters.
Their clothes were rags, their food meager, and their luxuries nonexistent.

The swan felt sad that they had so little and he had so much.

The mother grew impatient for the feathers and decided to take them all at once!

The next time the swan visited, she grabbed hold of him and plucked at his feathers.

The daughters wept and the swan cried out, but still the mother plucked.

The pile of glittering feathers grew and grew . . .

until the last swan feather was plucked. Then, all of a sudden, the pile of glittering feathers started to turn a dull brown until not one golden feather remained.

The mother and her daughters gasped in horror, but it was too late. The swan took his leave of the ungrateful woman, who had returned his generosity with such greed. He went with his friends to live in a far distant land, never to return to the little shack again.

Raktamukha was charmed by the invitation and gaily jumped on Karalamukha's back.
And so the pair set off toward the crocodile's home.

Not until the water grew deep did Karalamukha confess that he was going to kill Raktamukha
so that his wife could eat his heart. Raktamukha was horrified, but he kept his wits about him.
He begged Karalamukha to turn around, saying he had left his heart in the jamun tree.

# The Foolish Lion

So every day a forest animal was sent to King Bhasuraka's den, never to return.
Bhasuraka found that this system suited him very well and made him feel extremely kingly.

Now, the day came when it was the turn of a wise old rabbit to serve himself up for supper.
Old as he was, he was not a bit happy about being eaten. So he hopped very slowly
toward Bhasuraka's den, wondering how he might avoid his fate.

By the time Wise Old Rabbit reached the lion's den, Bhasuraka was roaring with impatience. When he saw the skinny old rabbit appear, he roared even louder!

Wise Old Rabbit apologized profusely for his lateness and his smallness. He explained that he had set out with five companions but that another lion, who also claimed to be king of the forest, had eaten them. When King Bhasuraka heard this, he exploded with rage and swore to tear the impostor to shreds!

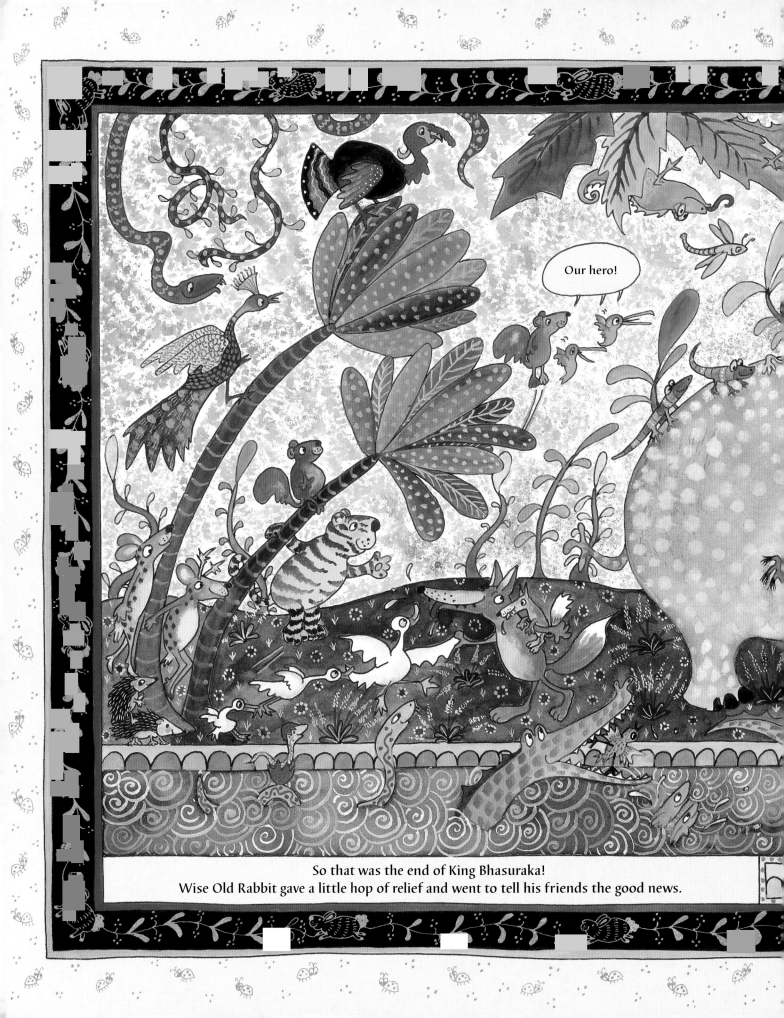

So that was the end of King Bhasuraka!
Wise Old Rabbit gave a little hop of relief and went to tell his friends the good news.

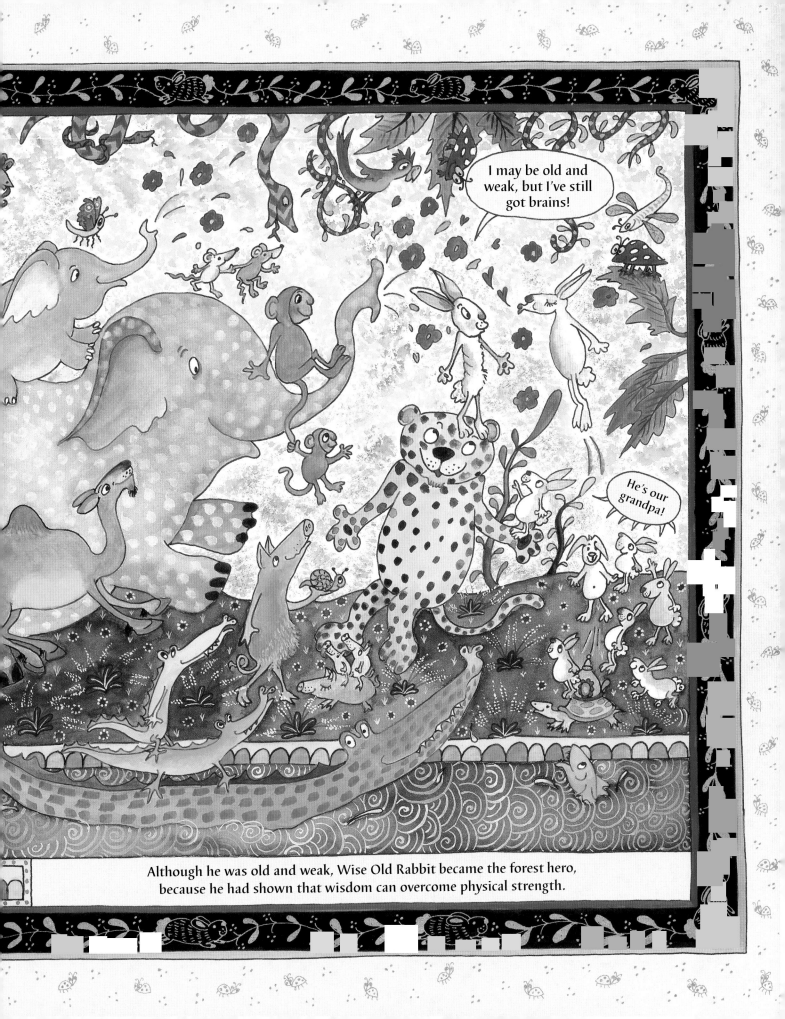

Although he was old and weak, Wise Old Rabbit became the forest hero,
because he had shown that wisdom can overcome physical strength.

First U.S. paperback edition 2014

Library of Congress Cataloging-in-Publication Data is available.
Library of Congress Catalog Card Number 2011048369
ISBN 978-0-7636-5916-5 (hardcover)
ISBN 978-0-7636-7055-9 (paperback)

16 17 18 CCP 10 9 8 7 6 5

Printed in Shenzhen, Guangdong, China

This book was typeset in Barbedor and Ondine
and hand-lettered by Kate Slater.
The illustrations were done in gouache and ink.

Candlewick Press
99 Dover Street
Somerville, Massachusetts 02144

visit us at www.candlewick.com

**Marcia Williams** has written and illustrated many books in her highly successful and entertaining comic-strip style. Among her many retellings are *Ancient Egypt: Tales of Gods and Pharaohs*, *Greek Myths*, and *Tales from Shakespeare*. About *The Elephant's Friend*, she says, "I had great fun following these animals along their strange and exotic paths. I met sights, sounds, and smells previously unknown to me, but the creatures themselves seemed familiar. Their passions, disappointments, triumphs, and foibles could have been my own . . . or maybe yours!" Marcia Williams lives in London.